This book belongs to
Eva

Bluebell Glade

Dandelion Dell

Heart of Misty Wood

Hawthorn Hedgerows

How many Fairy Animals books have you collected?

- Chloe the Kitten
- Bella the Bunny
- Paddy the Puppy
- Mia the Mouse
- Poppy the Pony
- Hailey the Hedgehog
- Sophie the Squirrel
- Daisy the Deer

And there are more magical adventures coming very soon!

Fairy Animals
of Misty Wood

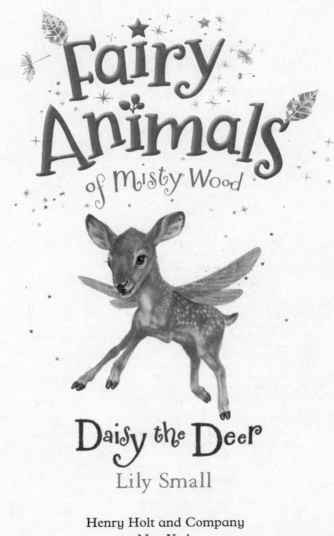

Daisy the Deer

Lily Small

Henry Holt and Company
New York

With special thanks to Susannah Leigh

Henry Holt and Company
Publishers since 1866
175 Fifth Avenue
New York, NY 10010
mackids.com

First published in the United States in 2017 by Henry Holt and Company.
Originally published in Great Britain in 2014 by Egmont UK Limited.

Library of Congress Cataloging-in-Publication Data

Names: Small, Lily, author.
Title: Daisy the deer / Lily Small.
Description: New York : Henry Holt and Company, 2017 | Series: Fairy animals of
   Misty Wood | Summary: Daisy the Dream Deer loves flying around in the moonlight,
   whispering happy dreams into the ears of the sleeping fairy animals, but when she
   comes across a little hedgehog who is too scared to sleep, can Daisy persuade him
   that there is nothing to be afraid of in Misty Wood?
Identifiers: LCCN 2016020539 (print) | LCCN 2016046483 (ebook) | ISBN
   9781627797382 (pbk.) | ISBN 9781627797399 (Ebook)
Subjects: | CYAC: Fairies—Fiction. | Deer—Fiction. | Hedgehogs—Fiction. |Animals—
   Fiction. | Dreams--Fiction. | Fear of the dark—Fiction. | Bedtime—Fiction.
Classification: LCC PZ7.S6385 Dai 2014 (print) | LCC PZ7.S6385 (ebook) | DDC
   [Fic]—dc23
LC record available at https://lccn.loc.gov/2016020539

Our books may be purchased in bulk for promotional, educational, or business use.
Please contact your local bookseller or the Macmillan Corporate
and Premium Sales Department at (800) 221-7945 ext. 5442
or by e-mail at MacmillanSpecialMarkets@macmillan.com.

First American Edition—2017
Printed in the United States of America by
LSC Communications, Harrisonburg, Virginia

9   10

Contents

CHAPTER ONE

Sweet Dreams, Misty Wood

It had been a beautiful day in
Misty Wood, and now the sun was
ready to go to sleep. As the sky

turned from bright blue to deepest
purple, the stars began to twinkle
and the moon climbed to join them.
Down below, the Bud Bunnies were
curled up in their cozy burrows, the
Pollen Puppies' tails had stopped
wagging, and the Cobweb Kittens
snoozed in their mossy beds.

But not *everyone* was asleep.
Oh no. Some fairy animals were
just waking up! They were sniffing
the cool evening air, fluttering their
wings, and thinking about their
special jobs, which made Misty
Wood such a wonderful place to
live.

On the banks of Moonshine Pond, the Moonbeam Moles had already popped out of their tunnels and were bustling about gathering their nets. Soon, they'd all be busy collecting moonbeams to drop into the pond so that it would glisten and shine.

Over on Sundown Hill, a Dream Deer called Daisy was stretching her long, slender legs. She blinked her big brown eyes,

smoothed her pale blue fur, and flexed her silvery wings. Daisy's special job was to fly around the wood at night, delivering wonderful dreams to the sleeping fairy animals.

"I think I have the best job of *all*!" Daisy sighed happily. She bounded to the top of Sundown Hill and gazed at Misty Wood. Usually it was very quiet at night, but tonight the wind was rushing

around, making the grass whisper
and the trees rustle. Leaves whirled
this way and that. But Daisy didn't
mind. She spread her wings and the
breeze caught them, lifting her into
the air.

"Wheeeee!" she cried as a gust
blew her toward Golden Meadow.
"It's going to be fun, flying in the
wind tonight!"

She landed lightly at the edge
of Golden Meadow, where the

flowers ended and the trees began.
"Time to start work!" she said.

She trotted slowly along a little
pathway that snaked between the
trees, looking out for any sleeping
fairy animals. It wasn't long before
she caught sight of some little white
whiskers and cute pointy ears,
tucked into a cozy nook in a tree
trunk.

"I know those ears," Daisy
whispered with a smile.

They belonged to Connie the Cobweb Kitten, one of Daisy's friends. Connie was fast asleep. Daisy tiptoed closer, then poked her soft nose into Connie's snug, warm home. The little kitten would receive Daisy's first dream of the night!

"You've just left Dewdrop Spring, where you collected a big basket of dewdrops," whispered Daisy in the kitten's velvety ear. "There are enough to hang on *all*

the cobwebs in Misty Wood, to make them sparkle and shine! And then you see a big bowl of fresh cream."

Connie's button nose twitched

in her sleep, and she gave a tiny, happy meow.

"It looks delicious," Daisy went on, "but you're not sure if it's for you. Then you see a name on the bowl—*CONNIE*. It *is* for you!"

Connie licked her lips with her little pink tongue, and she began to purr. Daisy smiled and crept away, knowing that Connie would enjoy her bowl of cream for the whole night.

11

Daisy leaped elegantly into the air and let the wind carry her toward Moonshine Pond. Above the water, the Moonbeam Moles flitted back and forth, catching moonbeams in their nets. Daisy couldn't be sure, but they looked as though they were working doubly hard tonight.

She spotted a pretty mole with rich purple fur and silver-gray wings.

12

"Yoo-hoo, Maddy!" she called, cantering along the bank.

Maddy was Daisy's best friend. Sometimes, when they'd both finished their work for the night, they would go off together to play in the meadows. It was lovely to share the moonlight with a friend when all the other animals were asleep.

Maddy swooped and landed next to Daisy, waving her net.

13

"Hello, Daisy!" she said, sounding a bit out of breath. "I'm really sorry, but I can't stop and chat tonight."

Daisy glanced up at all the moles whipping to and fro in the wind. "Why? What's going on? You all look so busy."

"Yes," said Maddy, her dark eyes shining. "We're having a competition. And you'll never guess—the first prize is a yummy

14

dessert. A big brambleberry crumble!"

"Ooooh," Daisy gasped, her mouth watering. "Brambleberry crumble's my favorite!"

Maddy smiled. "Mine too!"

"So, what do you have to do for your competition?" asked Daisy.

"The first mole to collect one hundred moonbeams wins," Maddy explained.

"One hundred? That's loads!"

15

Daisy exclaimed. "Do you think

you can do it?"

Maddy peered into her net.

"I'm doing *quite* well," she said.

"I've already got about twenty. I'd better keep going because I really, really want to win."

"Yes, of course." Daisy nodded. "I'll come back to see you later. Good luck!"

Daisy watched as Maddy took off, whizzing after a moonbeam with her net. She soon caught it, and Daisy grinned. Maddy had a good chance of winning—she was so determined. All the same, Daisy

17

felt glad she didn't have such an energetic job to do. Hers was much more peaceful. She opened her wings and flew off toward Heather Hill, where she was sure she'd find plenty of sleeping animals to whisper dreams to.

At the foot of the hill stood some old oak trees. Their twisting roots made lots of nooks and crannies that were perfect for fairy animals to sleep in. As Daisy drew closer, she

18

spotted a small bundle curled up on some leaves. She floated down to see who it might be.

"A Hedgerow Hedgehog!" she exclaimed to herself as she landed beside him. "Now, I wonder what sort of dream he'd like?"

She thought for a moment, then bent down to whisper in the little hedgehog's ear. But just as she was about to begin, he jumped up, his prickles spiking

19

out in all directions. Daisy leaped
back quickly, before a spike could
hurt her nose. The hedgehog
started running around in circles,
flapping his russet-red wings.

"Hey," Daisy called. "I thought
you were asleep!"

The hedgehog stopped running
and looked up at her with sad,
fearful eyes. "No," he said. "I
wasn't. I'm awake."

"I can see that," said Daisy.

"But you're a hedgehog, and hedgehogs aren't supposed to stay up all night! You must be so tired from tidying up leaves all day. I was just about to give you a lovely dream."

The hedgehog's bottom lip began to quiver. "I don't want a dream," he said in a wobbly voice.

Daisy stared at him. "But everyone *loves* dreams."

The hedgehog shook his head.

"Well, I don't. And I don't want to sleep." He stamped his tiny foot. "In fact, I'm never going to sleep. Never, ever, EVER again!"

CHAPTER TWO

The Hedgehog Gobbler

"Never?" Daisy's big brown eyes opened wide.

"No, never!" the hedgehog cried. He curled up in a ball and

24

began to sob. "And you can't make me!" came his muffled voice.

"It's okay," Daisy said softly. "Don't worry. I won't try to make you sleep. But will you tell me your name?"

"I'm H-H-Herbie," the hedgehog stammered.

"Hello, Herbie. I'm Daisy." She sat down beside him. "So, why don't you want to sleep?"

A fat tear rolled down Herbie's

cheek. "Because of the Hedgehog Gobbler."

Daisy stared at him in astonishment. "The . . . what?"

"The Hedgehog Gobbler!" cried Herbie. "He's a horrible monster that comes and gobbles up hedgehogs while they sleep! He creeps up from behind, and then he opens his big mouth with its rows of jaggedy teeth and . . . *chomp!* He gobbles you up."

Daisy frowned. "I've never heard

of a Hedgehog Gobbler before."

"Well, he's around here

somewhere," Herbie said, peering

27

over his shoulder. "He could pounce at any time. That's why I'm going to stay awake forever from now on. I'm never going to go to sleep and let him catch me!"

Daisy tried to remember all the different creatures that she knew lived in Misty Wood. There were Moss Mice and Bud Bunnies and Petal Ponies and Pollen Puppies. Cobweb Kittens, Moonbeam Moles, and Stardust Squirrels . . .

28

but she had never, ever heard of a Hedgehog Gobbler.

"I really don't believe there's such a thing as a Hedgehog Gobbler," she told Herbie in a gentle voice. "I think you should try to get to sleep, and then I'll give you a lovely dream that will help you forget all about it."

"But there *is*!" Herbie insisted. "So I *can't* sleep!" His bright eyes filled with tears again.

29

"All right, Herbie," Daisy said hurriedly. "But you're going to get awfully tired."

The hedgehog wiped away his tears with his tiny pink paw. "I won't get tired." He fluttered his wings and flew in a circle. "I'm wide awake—see?"

Daisy sighed. She could see that Herbie had made up his mind. But perhaps if he got *really* tired, he'd have to fall sleep. And she

30

knew she could definitely help him there. . . .

"Well, I have an idea," she told him. "If you're going to stay awake, how about you help me with my job?"

"What, delivering dreams?" Herbie asked, looking a bit more cheerful.

"That's right," said Daisy. "If you come with me, you'll have to fly around all night, so the Hedgehog Gobbler won't be able to find you."

Herbie started to grin. "Wow. I'd love to," he said. "I think you have an amazing job!"

"Well, yes, I do like it." Daisy smiled. "Come on, then. Let's head for Honeydew Meadow first."

They took off in a whirl of leaves. Herbie whooped with glee and chased after them. Daisy was pleased. The more energy the little hedgehog used up, the better. They dipped and dived, riding the breeze

32

THE HEDGEHOG GOBBLER

and enjoying the feel of the wind buffeting them to and fro.

When they reached the meadow, Daisy pointed down at a moss cushion surrounded with flowers, their buds shut tight for the night. On top of the cushion lay a Pollen Puppy, sound asleep.

"We'll start here," she told Herbie as they landed next to the puppy.

"So, what do we do?" Herbie

asked, his eyes shining with excitement.

"We'll think of all the things that a Pollen Puppy loves," she explained. "Then we'll whisper them into his ear."

"Ooooh. Well, I know they love juicy bones to chew," Herbie said eagerly. "And they love chasing one anothers' tails and scampering around the meadows flicking pollen and having fun."

Daisy nodded. "That's great, thank you," she said. "Now I can make a lovely dream for him."

She bent forward and began to murmur into the puppy's floppy ear. "You're having a wonderful time chasing your best friend's tail in Honeydew Meadow . . ." she began.

The Pollen Puppy's paws twitched, and his tail thumped against his mossy cushion.

"Look at him!" squeaked Herbie. "He's really enjoying it!"

Daisy smiled and carried on. "You're bounding past a horse chestnut tree when all of a sudden you spot a delicious bone. . . ."

The puppy gave a happy whine, and his ears pricked up in his sleep.

"The bone is big and juicy, so there's plenty for you to share," Daisy whispered. "You and your

friend have a lovely time, eating it and playing with it together!"

The puppy rolled over onto his back and wriggled in delight, his paws waving in the air. Daisy stepped back, proud of their work.

"That was fantastic!" He1 exclaimed as they slipped away "Can we do another one?"

Daisy grinned at him. "Of course!" she said. "Come on, let's go into the Heart of Misty Wood. Lots of fairy animals will be asleep in there."

They glided toward the center of the wood, then swooped down between the trees and began to flutter along near the ground,

39

watching for sleeping creatures.
Herbie was clearly enjoying every
minute, but he seemed to be getting
sleepy, too. His flying was getting
slower, and he gave a great big
yawn. Daisy slowed down as well,
feeling pleased. Her plan was
working! Soon Herbie would be so
tired he'd have to stop for a rest.
Then, when he'd dropped off, she'd
give him the best dream ever.

But suddenly Herbie cried out.

"Daisy!" he shouted. "Stop! Stop! It's the Hedgehog Gobbler!"

"What? Where?" Daisy whirled around in a circle.

"THERE!" Herbie pointed behind her with a trembling paw.

Daisy turned and gasped. Right ahead was an enormous towering figure. It was making an awful groaning sound—and it had HUGE waving arms!

CHAPTER THREE

The Night Fright

Daisy gulped. "Hide behind me," she said to Herbie, sounding a lot braver than she felt.

Herbie didn't need to be told

twice. He quickly scuttled behind Daisy.

Daisy took a deep breath and faced the figure. "Who are you?" she demanded.

"I told you—it's the Hedgehog Gobbler!" squealed Herbie.

Daisy tried to stay calm. *There's no such thing as a Hedgehog Gobbler*, she told herself firmly. Plucking up her courage, she took a step toward the huge creature.

"Careful, Daisy!" whimpered Herbie. "I know you're a deer, but it might get you, too!"

"Don't you worry, Herbie," Daisy told him. She peered forward to get a better look . . . then she sighed with relief. "It's not the Hedgehog Gobbler," she said, looking down at Herbie.

"It's not?" Herbie whispered.

Daisy smiled. "No. It isn't a monster at all. It's a tree!"

"What do you mean, a tree?" Herbie huffed, sticking out his prickles. "It can't be. It's got arms!"

"There's nothing here to hurt you," Daisy assured him. "I promise. Come on. Come and see."

Herbie peeked around Daisy's legs. Sure enough, all that stood before them was a big old beech tree. Its trunk was shadowy in the moonlight. The "arms" were its branches waving wildly in the wind,

THE NIGHT FRIGHT

47

and the groaning sound was just its roots creaking.

Herbie's prickles began to calm down. "Oh yes," he said happily. "Silly me. It *is* just a tree."

He scampered forward and skipped all the way around the trunk, clapping his wings together as he went. Daisy sighed. At least Herbie felt safe again, for now—but the trouble was, being frightened by the tree had really woken him

up. Now he didn't look the least bit sleepy.

"Let's go somewhere else, Herbie," Daisy suggested. "I think the trees look a bit too scary in the moonlight. We'll go to Hawthorn Hedgerows instead."

"Good idea," said Herbie, fluttering along next to her. "Lots of Moss Mice sleep there."

"Will you help me find one?" Daisy asked.

49

Herbie puffed out his chest proudly. "Of course."

Sure enough, it didn't take Herbie very long to find a tiny Moss Mouse curled up in a cozy nest of twigs and moss.

"Well done," said Daisy. "You're being a big help. Now, let's think. What do Moss Mice like?"

"Poppy seeds," Herbie said at once. "And hawthorn berries. I think they like *my* favorite food,

too—yummy hazelnuts. And they love being all together, having fun with their families and friends."

Daisy nodded. "Thank you. That's plenty to work with." She bent down to make a perfect dream for the mouse.

"It's your birthday," Daisy whispered into his tiny ear.

The mouse's nose and whiskers twitched in excitement.

"All your friends are here, and

your whole family, too," Daisy
continued. "Everyone's having a
lovely time. Your mom has made a
delicious hawthorn-berry pie, and
there's hazelnut cake for later."

"Yum!" Herbie exclaimed, rubbing his tummy. "Make sure they all sing a song," he added. "I love it when fairy animals sing songs at parties."

Daisy smiled and nodded. "Everyone eats piles of poppy seed pancakes," she whispered to the mouse. "Then they all sing 'Happy Birthday' to you. It's your best birthday party ever!"

They watched as the mouse

53

gave a little squeak of happiness
in his sleep, and then they tiptoed
away. Another good job done!

Daisy led Herbie to Dandelion
Dell, where the flower heads were
closed up for the night. The stems
were rocking to and fro in the
breeze. "Are you tired yet?" she
asked the little hedgehog. She was
quite sure that he must be by now.

"Not a bit," said Herbie.
"I'm getting hungry, though.

And thirsty." He looked at Daisy hopefully. "Where do you think we should go next?"

Daisy sighed. How was she ever going to get Herbie to sleep?

"Let's go to Moonshine Pond," she said. "You can have a drink there. And maybe we'll find a snack on the way."

As they started flapping their wings, a big gust of wind whisked them both up into the air. Herbie

55

did a loop-the-loop as the breeze lifted him.

"Wheeeee!" he yelled as he zoomed past Daisy, upside down.

Daisy dived after him, laughing, then chased him all the way across the meadows and dells. As they swung around a clump of bushes, she spotted something dangling in the moonlight.

"Herbie!" she called. "Come back here!"

Herbie did a somersault in the air to turn around.

"You said you were hungry, didn't you?" asked Daisy.

"Yes, I'm starving!" Herbie said, zooming up.

"And I think you said that you love hazelnuts?"

"Ooooh, yes," Herbie cried. "They're my favorite. Why, have you found some?"

"A whole bush of them,"

said Daisy. "And they're just ripe enough to eat!"

Quickly, they gathered a little pile of nuts, and Daisy helped Herbie crack them open with a stamp of her hoof. Herbie chomped his way through half of them, and then stopped.

"I'm full now," he sighed, rubbing his tummy. "But I could really use a drink."

"No problem," Daisy said,

launching herself into the air again.

"We're not far from the pond now."

Above Moonshine Pond, the

Moonbeam Moles were still hard

at work, gathering moonbeams as

fast as they could. While Herbie swooped down to the banks of the pond to slurp the crystal-clear water, Daisy looked around for her friend Maddy. She flew over the pond, weaving in and out of all the busy moles, but there was no sign of her.

"That's strange," muttered Daisy. "Where has Maddy gone? Surely she's still here catching moonbeams?"

And then, just as Herbie flew up to join her again, she spotted Maddy—all alone on the banks of the pond, standing by a clump of bullrushes.

"There's my friend," she told Herbie. "Let's go and talk to her!"

As they fluttered down to land beside Maddy, Daisy's heart gave a little thud. She could tell right away that something was wrong. Maddy was looking very gloomy. Her

silver-gray wings were drooping and her velvety fur looked flat.

"Maddy, what's wrong?" asked Daisy.

Maddy gave a loud sniff. "There's been a disaster," she said in a trembly voice. "A *total* disaster, in fact!"

CHAPTER FOUR

The Lost Moonbeams

"A disaster!" Daisy exclaimed.
"What's happened?" Then she
noticed something was missing.
"Maddy, where's your net?"

"That's the disaster," said Maddy, a tear trickling down her nose. "I was just chasing a lovely big moonbeam when the wind came along and blew my net away—*whoooosh!*"

"Oh no!" Daisy felt so sorry for her friend. Maddy had been working really hard.

"It was nearly full, too." Maddy sat down and buried her face in her paws.

"But that's not so bad, is it?"

Herbie asked, looking puzzled.

"Can't you get another net?"

Maddy gave a little sob. "Yes,

but—but not tonight. Not in time to

win the competition." She quickly explained the rules to Herbie. "And I was so close! I almost had a hundred moonbeams and now they're all lost!" A tear rolled down her face, and she wiped it way with her paw.

"Oh, Maddy, please don't cry. We'll help you look for it," Daisy said kindly. "It can't have gone too far. Herbie here will help, won't you, Herbie?"

"Of course I will." Herbie gave a little skip of excitement. "I love hunting for things. Hide-and-seek is my most favorite game ever."

Maddy peeked at them from between her paws. She was looking a teeny bit hopeful now. "Would you?" she asked.

"Yes! Come on, let's go—there's no time to lose!" cried Daisy.

Herbie was already up in the air with his wings spread, riding

68

circles on the wind. "Let's look in trees first!" he yelled.

He shot off at full speed with Daisy and Maddy just behind. The branches of the trees were swinging, their leaves jostling and rustling, but there was no sign of Maddy's net. So they flew on toward some small bushes on the other side of Moonshine Pond. Herbie dived under them and whizzed over them, but there was still no sign of the net.

DAISY THE DEER

"Now where can we look?" wailed Maddy. "I'll never find it. And I'll never win the contest and get my brambleberry crumble!"

But then Herbie glanced up. "What's that?" he cried, his prickles on end. He looked at Daisy, his eyes wide with fear. "Is it—is it—the Hedgehog Gobbler?"

Daisy followed his gaze and gasped. There was something very strange among the stars! A

mysterious glowing light, traveling quickly across the sky.

"No, no, no, that's not the Hedgehog Gobbler," she reassured him.

"Yes, it is," Herbie said, flying around in fright. "Those are his big scary eyes, glowing at us."

"I told you, there's no such thing as the Hedgehog Gobbler," Daisy said firmly. "Shall we go and see what it really is?"

"Only if you go first," Herbie said fearfully.

"Okay, come on, then!" Daisy called. She launched off with Maddy and Herbie on her tail.

Up, up, up they flew, over the trees and high above the Heart of Misty Wood. The glowing object was still ahead of them, whirling and dancing in the wind. Daisy beat her wings even harder, until finally she got close enough to see

73

what it was. And when she did, she couldn't believe her eyes!

"Maddy, it's your net!" she called. "It's glowing because it's so full of moonbeams!"

Daisy rushed after it, but Maddy and Herbie were struggling to keep up. Their little wings were whirring, and they were out of breath already!

"Please . . . can . . . you . . . catch it . . . Daisy?" Maddy gasped. "Your wings . . . are bigger . . . than ours."

74

"I'll do my best!" Daisy cried.
She surged forward after the
net. The wind whipped through
her pale blue fur and made her
brown eyes water, but she tucked
her head down and flew faster,
faster, faster—faster than she'd ever
flown before! Maddy's net spun
and twisted through the air, turning
cartwheels as it shot over the dark
trees of the wood. Daisy swished
this way and that, following the net

as it flew above the treetops and headed toward Dewdrop Spring.

Daisy beat her wings even faster. Now she was close enough to see all the different moonbeams glistening inside the net. She hoped none of them had fallen out.

"One more push!" she said to herself.

Closer . . . closer . . . closer! She reached out with her long neck, trying to catch the net between her

78

teeth. But just as she was about to catch it, the wind snatched it and sent it spiraling toward Dewdrop Spring.

"Oh no! It mustn't land in the water!" Daisy cried. "We'll never get the moonbeams back if it does."

She dived down, swooping toward the surface of the spring. The wind suddenly dropped, and the net began to fall down . . . down . . . down. . . .

"I'm going to be too late!" Daisy puffed.

She flapped her wings as hard as she could and zoomed after it. She wouldn't give up! As she opened her mouth to grab the net with her teeth, she heard a big *SPLASH*. She'd gotten it! But what was that splash? Had the moonbeams fallen out?

CHAPTER FIVE

A Special Visitor

Daisy rose up away from Dewdrop
Spring and circled around to find
Maddy and Herbie, who were just
catching up.

"You did it!" Maddy cheered.

"Yes," said Daisy, passing her the net. "But I'm really sorry—I think I lost some of your moonbeams. I heard them splashing into the water."

"No, no," squealed Herbie. "We saw it all. It wasn't the moonbeams that splashed into the water—it was your hooves!"

Daisy felt her heart leap. She was so relieved!

"Thank you, thank you!" Maddy squeaked, fluttering around Daisy. "Now I'd better go and make up for lost time. Maybe I can still win the competition!"

"Yes, yes, go go go!" Daisy exclaimed. "And good luck!"

As Maddy raced off, Daisy looked down. Her legs and hoofs were dripping with water, so she shook them one by one to dry them, then turned to Herbie.

"You *must* be tired by now, Herbie," she said. "That was a lot of flying, wasn't it?"

Herbie's eyes were beginning to droop. He put one paw up to his mouth to hide a yawn. "Yes, it was. But I'm not tired." He blinked, then tried to open his eyes wide. "Not even a tiny bit."

"Are you sure?" Daisy asked gently. "Wouldn't you like to snuggle down to sleep?"

"No! I told you—I'm never

going to sleep again," Herbie

insisted, hiding another yawn.

Daisy gave her fur one last

85

shake, and smiled. "Oh yes, you did say that. Well, we'd better do something else, then. How about we go back to Heather Hill?"

Herbie looked at her suspiciously. "But that's where I usually go to sleep for the night," he said. "You're not going to make me go to bed, are you?"

"No, no, of course not," Daisy said soothingly. "I need to find some more fairy animals to deliver

dreams to, that's all. You can help
me do that."

Herbie nodded. "All right,
then."

Daisy sniffed the cool air and
fluttered her wings. It was her
favorite time of night. The stars
were twinkling merrily, and the
moon was at its brightest. It was
when she felt her most lively—but
she could see that poor Herbie was
struggling. As they took off once

more, his wings would only beat
very slowly—so slowly that he
could hardly stay in the air!

"It's not too far," Daisy said.

"We'll fly back up past Golden Meadow, and you can have a rest every now and then if you want."

"I . . . don't . . . need . . . to . . . rest," said Herbie, but even his voice sounded slow.

Daisy felt so sorry for him. She wished he would believe that there was no such thing as a Hedgehog Gobbler, but he was much too frightened. What could she do?

They flew up the valley, past tall, waving poplar trees, gnarled old oaks, and blossoming hedgerows. They were about halfway up when Daisy thought she heard a strange whooshing sound. She glanced at Herbie. Could it be his tired wings making a funny noise?

But then Herbie heard it, too. "What's that noise?" he demanded. "Is it the Hedgehog Gobbler?"

The whooshing was getting louder, and louder, and LOUDER!

"It is!" Herbie yelled. "It really is the Gobbler this time!"

Daisy didn't know what to say. The whooshing sound was definitely very strange and scary, and she didn't know *what* it could be. She gestured at Herbie to fly down to the ground.

"Here it comes!" shrieked Herbie, making Daisy jump.

They cowered as a huge creature flew toward them. It had massive dark wings and enormous eyes. Even Daisy was frightened this time—it definitely wasn't a tree or a net of flying moonbeams!

"Who are you?" she called out bravely.

The creature swooped past them and landed on the branch of a sycamore tree. "I am the Wise Wishing Owl," it hooted.

"And tell me, whoooooooo are yooooooou?"

Daisy and Herbie heaved a sigh of relief, then looked at each other in amazement. The Wise Wishing Owl? She was the oldest, wisest creature in all of Misty Wood, and the fairy animals rarely saw her!

"I thought you were the Hedgehog Gobbler!" exclaimed Herbie. "I'm so glad you're not."

The Wise Wishing Owl ruffled

93

DAISY THE DEER

94

her feathers. "The Hedgehog what?" she hooted.

"The Hedgehog Gobbler," said Herbie, fluttering up toward the beautiful owl. "It's really big, even bigger than you, and ten times scarier," he explained breathlessly. "It's got huge teeth and a ginormous belly, and it comes out at night to find hedgehogs who are curled up fast asleep. And then it gobbles them up whole!"

"Is that so?" the Wise Wishing Owl said, gazing at him with her big round eyes.

"Yes! Yes!" said Herbie. "We've been trying to escape from it all night!"

"Oh, dear." The Wise Wishing Owl looked at Herbie gravely. "Tell me something, young hedgehog. I have lived in Misty Wood longer than any other creature, but I have never, ever heard of or seen a

Hedgehog Gobbler. So how do you explain that?"

"I don't know." Herbie frowned. "But I do know that he's out there

and that I mustn't ever go to sleep again."

The Wise Wishing Owl gave a soft chuckle. "All right," she said. "Tell me something else. Who told you about the Hedgehog Gobbler?"

"My big brother, Horace," said Herbie.

The Wise Wishing Owl nodded. "I thought it might be someone like that. Now, does Horace ever play tricks on you?"

"Oh yes," said Herbie. "We play tricks on each other all the time. He loves hiding my breakfast or jumping out at me from behind a tree, so then I pretend to be a spiny dragon to scare him or . . ." Suddenly, his eyes opened wide. "Do you—do you think the story about the Hedgehog Gobbler is one of his tricks?"

The Wise Wishing Owl smiled and nodded. "Yes, from what I

99

know about big brothers, I think
it most certainly is. Now, what
do you think he'd say if he knew
you'd stayed up all night worrying
about it?"

Herbie's cheeks went pink. "Oh!
He'd really laugh." He looked at
Daisy, then the owl, then back to
Daisy. "He'd better not find out."

"That's right," agreed the Wise
Wishing Owl, winking at Daisy.
Daisy smiled and nodded.

"In that case, I'd better get back to Heather Hill as fast as possible," said Herbie. "I've got a lot of sleeping to do!"

"Thank you, Wise Wishing Owl," said Daisy. "I'm so glad we've sorted out the mystery of the Hedgehog Gobbler at last!"

She and Herbie waved good-bye to the beautiful owl and rose up into the starry sky. Herbie managed to find one last burst of energy, and he

sailed along on the breeze singing to himself.

"There's no Hedgehog Gobbler," he warbled. "There's *nooo* Hedgehog Gobbler!"

Daisy chased after him, chuckling to herself, until Heather Hill was in sight. They swooped down to the old oak tree—the very same tree that she had found Herbie beside at the beginning of the night.

Herbie landed among the roots

and snuggled down. He curled into a ball, then looked up at Daisy with his eyelids drooping. "Thank you, Daisy," he said drowsily. "You've been a really good friend to me tonight."

"Oh, that's all right," said

Daisy. "You've been a big help to me, too. Perhaps we could have another adventure together one day."

But Herbie didn't reply. He had tucked his nose between his paws, and he was already fast asleep!

104

CHAPTER SIX

The Best Dream Ever

Daisy smiled to herself. "Now it's Herbie's turn for the best dream ever," she murmured. "Let's see . . ."

Daisy thought of all the things

she had learned about Herbie. She leaned close to his tiny ear and began. "You're out in the woods with your friends," she whispered. "You're all having loads of fun doing your special job, collecting leaves with your prickles to make Misty Wood nice and tidy. While you're working, you play hide-and-seek, and you hide so cleverly that no one can find you for the longest time!"

Daisy gazed down at Herbie and saw a happy smile curling up the corners of his mouth.

"And then, tucked into your hiding place, you spot something really tasty," she went on. "It's a big pile of shiny brown hazelnuts. When your friends find you at last, you show them what you've found and you all decide to have a hazelnut party!"

Herbie gave a tiny squeak of

107

excitement and twitched his nose in his sleep.

"You share all your hazelnuts with your friends and, to say thank you, they sing you a song. And then you all begin to dance."

As Herbie wriggled happily in his sleep, Daisy fetched some leaves to cover him so that he was even cozier than before. Then she slipped away quietly into the night, leaving him to his lovely dream.

With the moon beginning to
dip down in the sky, she knew she
had no time to waste—she wanted

to go and see how Maddy was
doing.

Daisy flew back down the
valley toward Moonshine Pond.
As she went, she realized that the
wind had finally dropped, and the
trees and hedgerows lay still and
silent under the sparkling stars.

*At least Maddy won't lose her net
now,* Daisy thought. *Maybe she'll
have managed to catch her final
moonbeams just in time.*

110

By the time she arrived at the pond, all the moles had finished work for the night. They were gathering on the banks by the willow trees, holding their moonbeam nets. The competition must be over already! Daisy rushed forward to see what was happening. Where was Maddy? And who had won?

And then she spotted her friend. She was standing right at

111

the top of the bank by a fallen tree trunk. Meredith, the oldest Moonbeam Mole of Misty Wood, was standing on the trunk as if it were a stage—and she was making an announcement.

"And the winner of our special brambleberry crumble competition is . . . Maddy!" she exclaimed. "Maddy, please step forward to show everyone your net!"

Maddy looked as though she

would burst with pride. She hopped onto the tree trunk and waved her net, which was bulging with all her moonbeams.

"Well done, Maddy. You were the first mole to collect one hundred moonbeams," Meredith said, smiling at her. "And now here's your special prize."

Daisy and all the moles clapped and cheered. Maddy bowed to everyone before accepting

DAISY THE DEER

the delicious dessert. The smell of
the crumble wafted over to Daisy,
and her mouth began to water. She
was so happy for her friend.

"Now, I know that Maddy
will be dying to taste her prize,"
said Meredith. "But first, there's
an important job to do. We have
all worked very, very hard tonight
collecting our moonbeams. And
now it's time to place them where
they belong—in Moonshine Pond.

So, Maddy, as our winner, would you please lead the way?"

Maddy nodded eagerly. She put her crumble down on the tree-trunk stage to keep it safe, then fluttered up and above the water with her net. She tilted the net and tipped out the moonbeams. They rippled gently into the water, lighting it up with a soft pearly glow. All the other Moonbeam Moles did the same, until

Moonshine Pond glistened and shimmered more beautifully than Daisy had ever seen before in her life. It looked amazing!

"Well done, Maddy!" Daisy called out.

"Daisy!" Maddy exclaimed happily, trotting back up the bank. "Come on—you have to help me eat my crumble!"

"Oh, no," said Daisy. "You won it—it's all yours!"

"Don't be silly," Maddy said with a smile. "If you hadn't caught my net for me, I never would have won. And anyway, there's far too much of it for just me."

Daisy grinned. "Well, if you're sure," she said. "Thank you!"

Together, they fetched the crumble and sat down by the trees to eat it. As Daisy took her first bite, she closed her eyes. It was the yummiest crumble ever.

"Mmmmmm," she mumbled.

"Mmmm-mmmm!" agreed
Maddy.

Their mouths were too full to
say anything else!

Daisy gazed over to the east, where the first hint of dawn was turning the sky from purple-black to deep blue. What a night of adventure it had been! As the crumble settled down into her tummy, she began to feel all warm and sleepy. She thought of Herbie enjoying his lovely dream, and smiled as she remembered how hard he'd tried to stay awake. Soon it would be bedtime for her, too,

but she was quite sure that she
wouldn't have Herbie's problem.
Oh no! She was so tired and
happy, it would only be seconds
before she was fast . . . asleep. . . .

Turn the page for

lots of fun

Misty Wood

activities!

Help Daisy Find
Maddy's Moonbeams!

Connect the Dots

Who is the special visitor?

Follow the numbers and connect all the dots to make a lovely picture from the story.

Start connecting with dot number 1. When you've finished joining all the dots, you can color in the picture!

Draw a Special Dream for Daisy

Daisy's special job is to give dreams to the sleeping fairy animals of Misty Wood.

But can you give Daisy a special dream while she is sleeping?

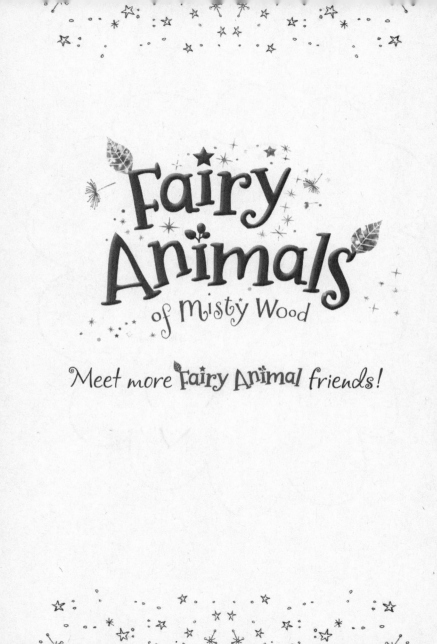

Fairy Animals
of Misty Wood

Meet more Fairy Animal friends!

Chloe the Kitten
Fun activities inside!
Fairy Animals
of Misty Wood
Lily Small

Bella the Bunny
Fun activities inside!
Fairy Animals
of Misty Wood
Lily Small

Paddy the Puppy
Fun activities inside!
Fairy Animals
of Misty Wood
Lily Small

Mia the Mouse
Fun activities inside!
Fairy Animals
of Misty Wood
Lily Small

Poppy the Pony
Fun activities inside!
Fairy Animals
of Misty Wood
Lily Small

Hailey the Hedgehog
Fun activities inside!
Fairy Animals
of Misty Wood
Lily Small

Sophie the Squirrel
Fun activities inside!
Fairy Animals
of Misty Wood
Lily Small

Daisy the Deer
Fun activities inside!
Fairy Animals
of Misty Wood
Lily Small